MR. MEN
The Great British Tour

Roger Hargreaves

Original concept by
Roger Hargreaves

Written and illustrated by
Adam Hargreaves

05265657

Little Miss Sunshine loves going on holiday. She likes nothing more than visiting new places with her friends. So, she bought a double decker bus to do her very own guided tour of Great Britain.

Sunshine Tours!

Little Miss Sunshine had bought everyone an umbrella for the trip. "It often rains in Britain," she laughed.

Mr Worry looked up at Little Miss Sunshine's bus.

"But your bus doesn't have a roof!" he cried.

"I know!" smiled Little Miss Sunshine. "All aboard!"

JOHN O'GROATS

LAND'S END

The Great British Tour was from Land's End in the most western corner of England to John O'Groats at the very top of Scotland.

The first stop on the tour was the Eden Project in Cornwall. In a huge dome, they trekked around a steamy rainforest and discovered how the plants there help keep us all alive.

Mr Greedy discovered how many cream teas he could eat!

Then they got back on the bus to travel to Wiltshire, where Little Miss Sunshine showed them Stonehenge. One of the wonders of the world and the most famous prehistoric monument in Britain.

Mr Worry stayed on the bus. Just in case it rained.

"Nobody knows how Neolithic man moved these enormous stones to build the circle," said Little Miss Sunshine.

"I think Mr Strong may have an idea," giggled Little Miss Giggles.

The next day, Little Miss Sunshine's tour took them across the south of England to Dover. Mr Worry was very concerned when he saw the hot air balloons which were going to take them over the White Cliffs.

"It's amazing – we're flying like a bird!" cried Little Miss Giggles. "I can even see France from up here!"

Luckily for Mr Worry, he was in Mr Greedy's balloon, which could not get off the ground.

Too many cream teas!

There was more tea at their next stop.

Mr Uppity had organised tea with the Queen at Windsor Castle!

Little Miss Splendid was very jealous when the Queen greeted Little Miss Princess like an old friend.

And Mr Worry was very scared of the corgis!

But things only went from bad to worse.

Little Miss Stubborn refused to curtsey in front of the Queen.

Mr Clumsy spilt his tea on the rug.

And, of course, Mr Greedy ate all the biscuits.

Mr Uppity was very embarrassed.

He wanted to be invited back!

After a stressful day at the castle, they decided to take things a bit slower and swap the bus for a barge along the Birmingham canals.

"Did you know that Birmingham has more canals than Venice?" asked Little Miss Sunshine. "Hop aboard, everyone!"

Mr Worry decided to stay on the bus again. He was worried he might fall off the barge.

And, of course, Mr Bump did fall in the canal.

And Mr Clumsy.

And Little Miss Whoops!

SPLASH!

Once they had all dried off, they climbed back on board Little Miss Sunshine's tour bus.

"Next stop, Wales!" cried Little Miss Sunshine.

"Did someone say whales?" asked Mr Worry, nervously looking over his shoulder.

But Mr Worry had no need to be worried, as they travelled out of England to Caernarfon Castle in Wales, where they watched an entertaining jousting competition.

Mr Topsy-Turvy was not going to win any prizes.

It was a flying visit to Wales, as that night they camped in Sherwood Forest under the stars. It was Mr Strong's idea that they dress up as Robin Hood and his merry band of outlaws.

Mr Mean made a very good Sheriff of Nottingham.

And Little Miss Somersault was an excellent shot with a bow and arrow.

Mr Dizzy was not so good.

Not so much a bow and arrow as an arrow and bow!

The next stop on Little Miss Sunshine's tour was Northern Ireland. They were up bright and early to board a ferry and sail across the Irish Sea.

Mr Tall wanted to see the Giant's Causeway.

Legend had it that long ago two giants loathed each other. Fionn, an Irish giant, built a path over the sea to reach the Scottish giant, Benandonner, but he ripped it up in a rage and the Giant's Causeway was made.

"However," explained Little Miss Sunshine, "the Causeway was really created by a volcano, 60 million years ago."

Mr Worry was not sure which version worried him more. Two giants or a volcano!

The following morning, they were back on the ferry to England for a relaxing day on Blackpool beach with fish and chips for lunch.

Mr Busy was too busy to stop for lunch. He was too busy making a sandcastle. It was nearly as tall as Blackpool Tower!

Which everyone climbed up after lunch.

Well, not everyone.

One person stayed on the ground.

And I'm sure you know who that was!

"Whales, giants, volcanos, heights, what next?" wondered Mr Worry.

Well, next was sailing on Coniston Water in the Lake District. They had hired a boat, but there was no wind.

Mr Worry's relief was short lived as Mr Strong had a lot of puff. He took a very deep breath and he huffed and he puffed and he puffed and he huffed all the way around the lake!

Mr Worry kept a close lookout for whales.

Little Miss Sunshine's tour was now nearing its end, but not before they travelled even further north through England up to Scotland. On their way, they passed the Angel of the North, which was four times taller than their double decker bus!

Just before they reached Scotland, they came to Hadrian's Wall, which was built by the Romans two thousand years ago.

They decided to go for a long walk, but Mr Forgetful forgot to shut one of the gates.

Poor Mr Worry.

He was even afraid of sheep!

BAAA!

In Scotland, they had to decide whether they should take the high road or the low road.

They decided on the high road.

All the way up Ben Nevis, the highest mountain in the British Isles. Mr Worry wished that he had not stayed on the bus this time!

After exploring Scotland, they finally reached John O'Groats. They all agreed it had been a wonderful tour.

"And we didn't even need the umbrellas," laughed Little Miss Sunshine, happily. "It's not called Sunshine Tours for nothing!"

Cautiously, Mr Worry stepped down from the bus.

PLOP!

"Was that a raindrop?" worried Mr Worry.

"No ..."

"… it was a seagull!" giggled Little Miss Giggles.